Heathers
The Musical

Book
Music and
Lyrics by
Kevin Murphy &
Laurence O'Keefe

Based on the
Film written by
Daniel Waters

Music & lyrics © 2015 by Kevin Murphy & Laurence O'Keefe
Title page logo & artwork designed by AKA NYC
Logo & artwork © 2012 by AKA NYC
ISBN: 978-0-573-70478-9

||| SAMUEL FRENCH |||

CONTENTS

BEAUTIFUL

Music and Lyrics by
Laurence O'Keefe and Kevin Murphy

VERONICA. September 1, 1989.

VERONICA. I think I'm a good person. I believe there's good in everyone.

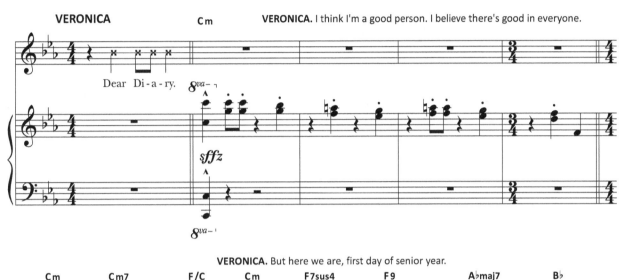

VERONICA. But here we are, first day of senior year.

VERONICA. I see these kids I've known all my life and wonder: What happened?

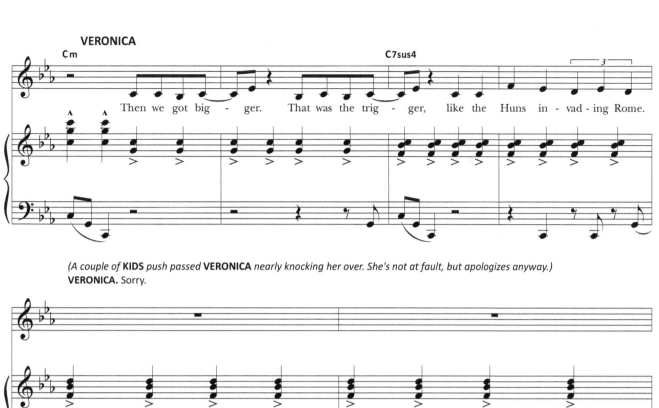

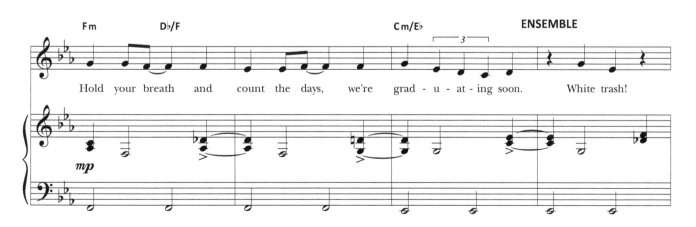

VERONICA

HIPSTER DORK VERONICA

VERONICA. You okay?
HIPSTER DORK. Get away, nerd.

VERONICA. Ram Sweeney. Third year as linebacker. And eighth year of smacking lunch trays and BEING A HUGE DICK.

RAM. What did you say to me, skank?

RAM. Oooooops.

VERONICA. ...Nothing.

VERONICA

But I___

Warmly

know,_____ I know..._____ Life can be beau - ti - ful. I

pray..._____ I pray..._____ For a bet - ter way.___ We were

kind be - fore;____ we can be kind once more.____ We can be___

8

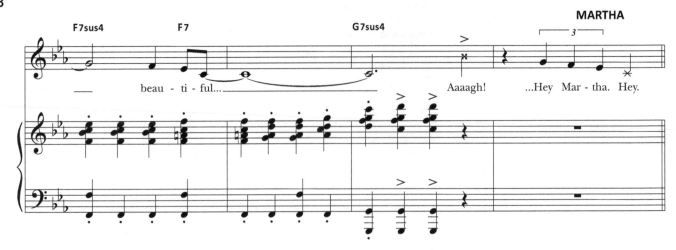

VERONICA. Martha Dunnstock. My
best friend since diapers. She's got a
huge heart. 'Round here, that's not
enough. *(to MARTHA)* Thanks.

MARTHA. We on for movie night?
VERONICA. You're on Jiffy Pop
detail.
MARTHA. I rented "The Princess Bride."
VERONICA. Again? Don't you have it
memorized by now?

MARTHA. What can I say? I'm a sucker for a happy ending.
KURT. Martha Dumptruck! Wide load! Honnnnnk!

VERONICA. Kurt Kelly. Quarterback. He is
the smartest guy on the football team.
Which is kind of like being the
tallest dwarf. *(to KURT)* Hey!
Pick that up right now!
KURT. I'm sorry, are you actually talking to me?
RAM. My buddy Kurt asked you a question.

VERONICA. What gives you the right to pick on my friend?
Look at you, you're a high school has-been waiting to happen.
A future gas station attendant.
KURT. You got a zit right there.

ENSEMBLE

God! Give me some hope___ here! Some-thing to live___

No rit. Non rubato

for!....

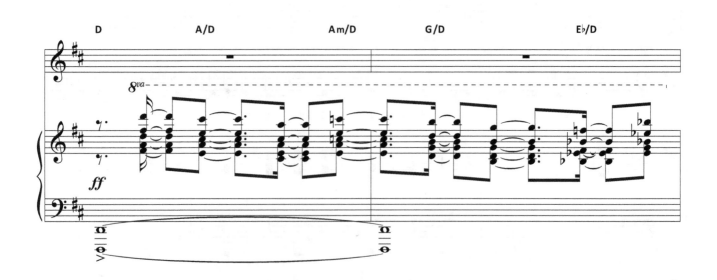

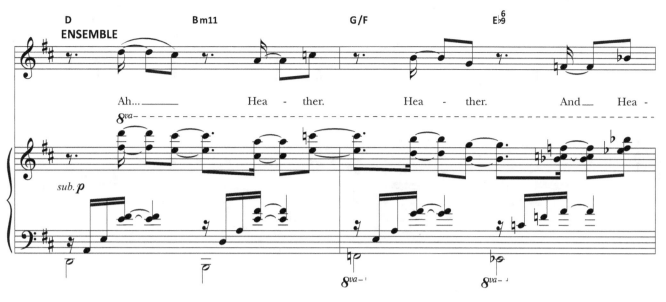

Ah._____ Hea - ther. Hea - ther. And_ Hea -

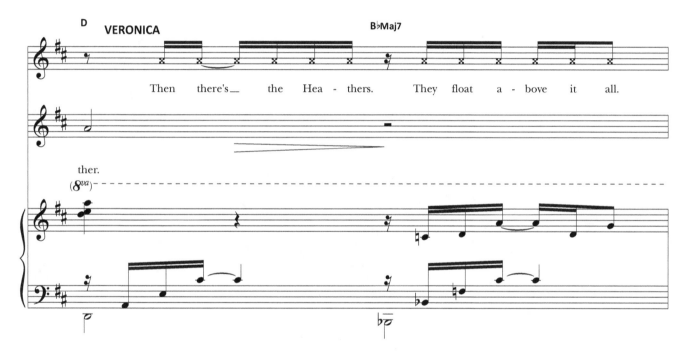

Then there's_ the Hea - thers. They float a - bove it all.

ther.

VERONICA. Heather McNamara. Head cheerleader. Her dad's loaded – he sells engagement rings.

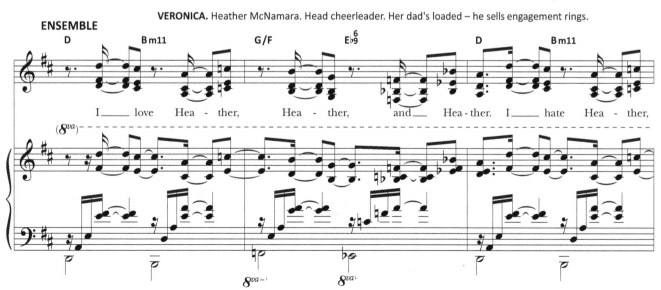

I_ love Hea - ther, Hea - ther, and_ Hea - ther. I_ hate Hea - ther,

VERONICA. Heather Duke. Runs the yearbook. Her parents sent her to Europe while her nose job healed.

Hea - ther, and ___ Hea - ther. I___ want Hea - ther,

VERONICA. And Heather Chandler. The Almighty.

VERONICA. She is a mythic bitch.

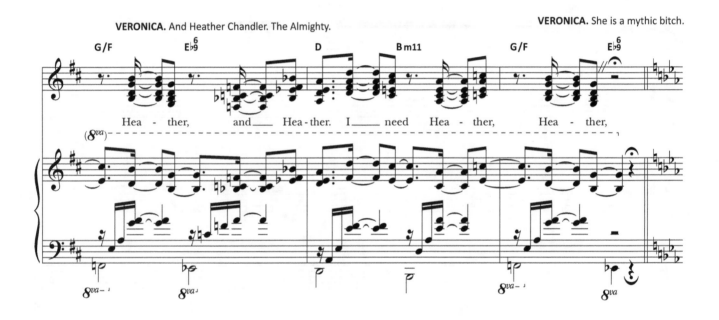

Hea - ther, and ___ Hea - ther. I ___ need Hea - ther, Hea - ther,

In 2, à la original "Beautiful" tempo; with some energy

VERONICA. They are solid Teflon — never bothered, never harassed. I would give anything to be like that.

Warm pop ballad feel

HIPSTER DORK. I'd like to be their boyfriend.

That would be beau - ti - ful.

STONER CHICK. If I sat at their table, guys would notice me.

Mm... So beau - ti - ful.

14

MARTHA. ...I'd like them to be nicer.

MARTHA

That would be beau - ti - ful.

Oo... That would be beau - ti - ful.

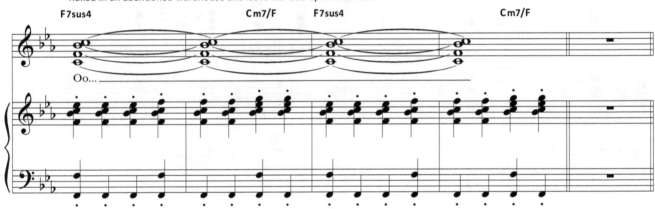

BELEAGUERED GEEK. I'd like to kidnap a Heather and photograph her naked in an abandoned warehouse and leave her tied up for the rats.

Oo...

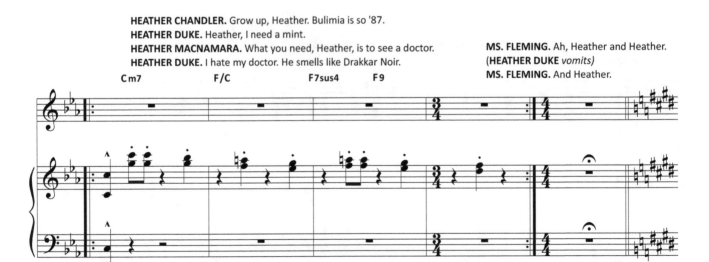

HEATHER CHANDLER. Grow up, Heather. Bulimia is so '87.
HEATHER DUKE. Heather, I need a mint.
HEATHER MACNAMARA. What you need, Heather, is to see a doctor.
HEATHER DUKE. I hate my doctor. He smells like Drakkar Noir.

MS. FLEMING. Ah, Heather and Heather.
(**HEATHER DUKE** *vomits*)
MS. FLEMING. And Heather.

MS. FLEMING. Perhaps you didn't hear
the bell over all the vomiting. You're late for class.
HEATHER CHANDLER. Heather wasn't
feeling well. We're helping her.

MS. FLEMING. Not without a hall pass you're not.
A week's detention.
VERONICA. Actually, Mrs. Fleming –

VERONICA. ...all four of us are
out on a hall pass. Yearbook committee.
(**VERONICA** hands **MS. FLEMING** a pass.)

MS. FLEMING. ...I see you're all listed.
Hurry up and get where you're going.

HEATHER CHANDLER. This is an excellent forgery.
Who are you?
VERONICA. Veronica Sawyer. I crave a boon.
HEATHER CHANDLER. What boon?
VERONICA. Let me sit at your table at lunch. Just once.
No talking necessary. If people think you guys tolerate me,
they'll leave me alone.

VERONICA. ...Before you answer: I also do report cards, permission slips, and absence notes.
HEATHER DUKE. How about prescriptions?
HEATHER CHANDLER. Shut up, Heather.
HEATHER DUKE. Sorry, Heather.

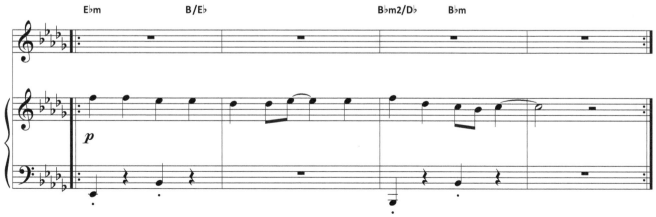

16

HEATHER CHANDLER. Hmm. For a greasy little nobody, you do have good bone structure.

HEATHER MCNAMARA. And a symmetrical face. If I took a meat cleaver down the center of your skull, I'd have matching halves. That's very important.
HEATHER DUKE. Of course, you could stand to lose a few pounds.

HEATHER CHANDLER

And ya know, ya know, ya know?... This could be beau - ti - ful. Mas - ca - ra, may - be some lip gloss... And we're on our way. Get this

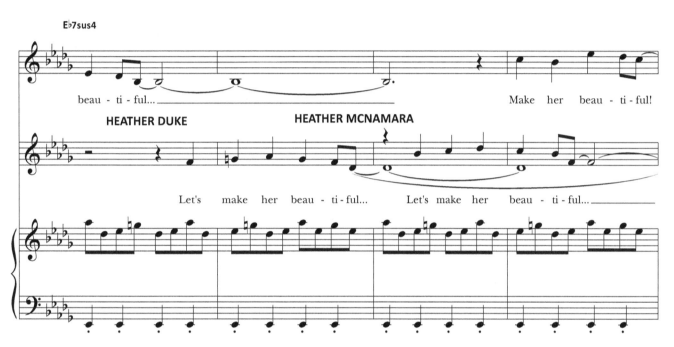

19

Faster and Bigger

MARTHA

babe! Hea - ther!... Hea - ther!... Hea - ther... Ve - ro - ni - ca?!

ENSEMBLE

Ve - ro - ni - ca? Ve - ro - ni - ca! VE - RO - NI -

VERONICA

CA!! And ya

It's a beau-ti-ful frick-in' day!

Hard Rock (2 feel)

C♯   G♯/C♯   G♯m/C♯   F♯/C♯

(day!)

Hea - ther! Hea - ther! Hea - ther! Ve ro - ni -

C♯   G♯/C♯   G♯m/C♯

Ad lib.

Hey!

ca! Hea - ther! Hea - ther!

CANDY STORE

Music and Lyrics by
Laurence O'Keefe and Kevin Murphy

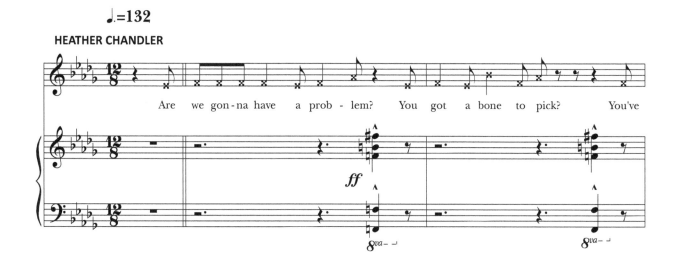

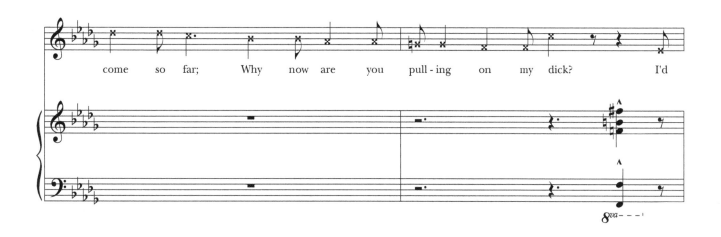

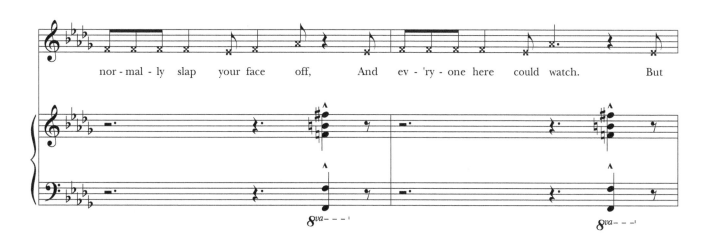

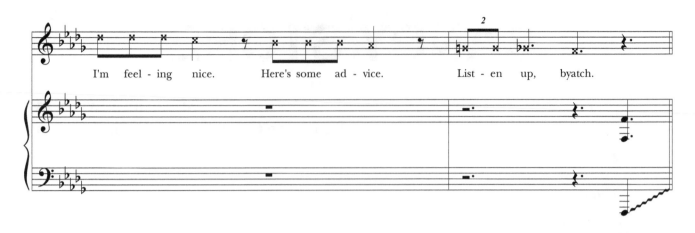

I'm feel - ing nice. Here's some ad - vice. List - en up, byatch.

Big Scary Stomping New Wave Rock

CHANDLER

I Like look-ing hot. Buy-ing stuff they can not. I Like drink ing hard. Max ing Dad's cred-it card.

DUKE, MAC, GALS

I Like   I Like

I Like skip ping gym. Scar ing her, screw ing him. I Like kil-ler clothes. Kick-ing nerds in the nose.

I Like   I Like

CHANDLER

If you lack the __ balls, __ you can go play dolls; __ let your mom-my fix you a snack.

DUKE and MCNAMARA

Whoa__ oh!

Or you could come smoke, __ Pound some rum and __ coke, __ In my Por-sche with the

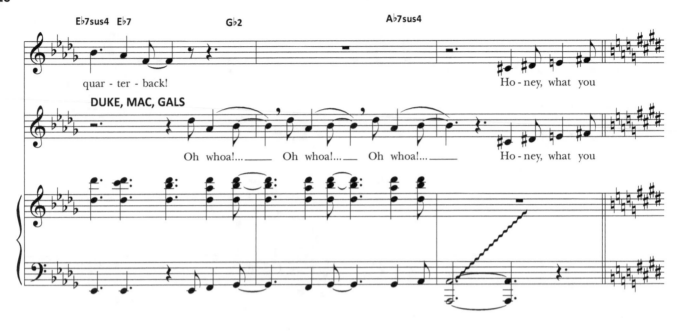

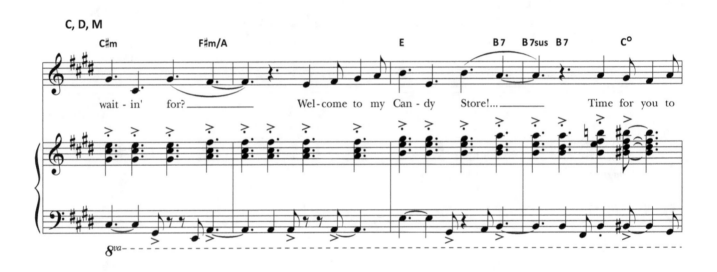

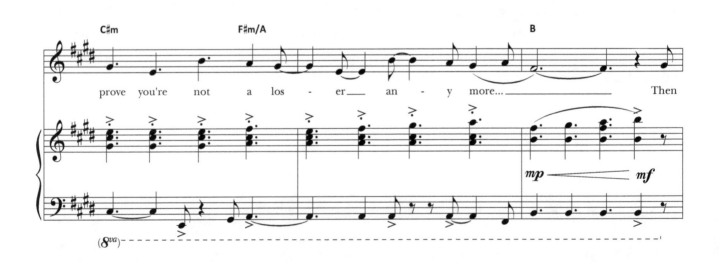

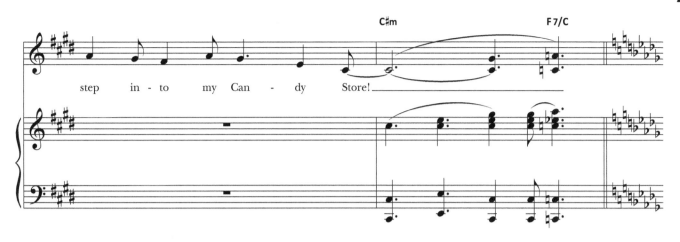

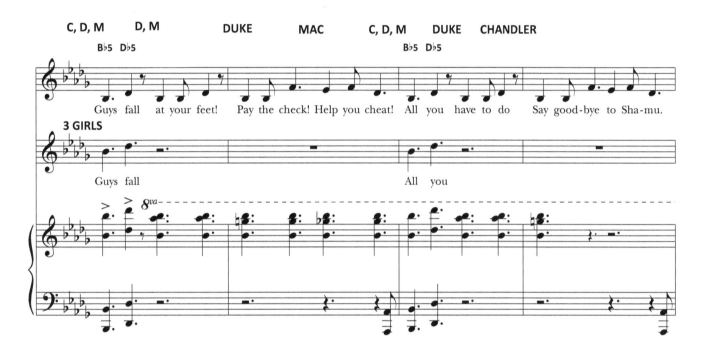

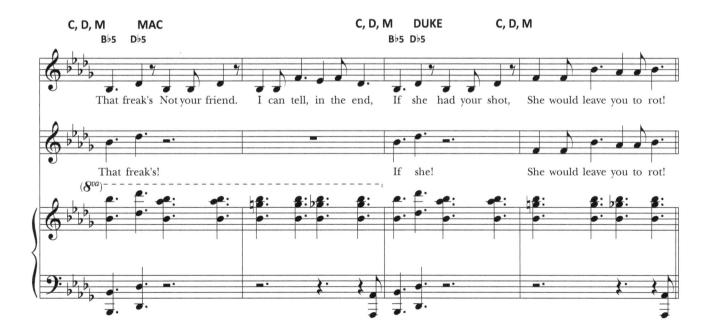

30

32

Reggae feel

33

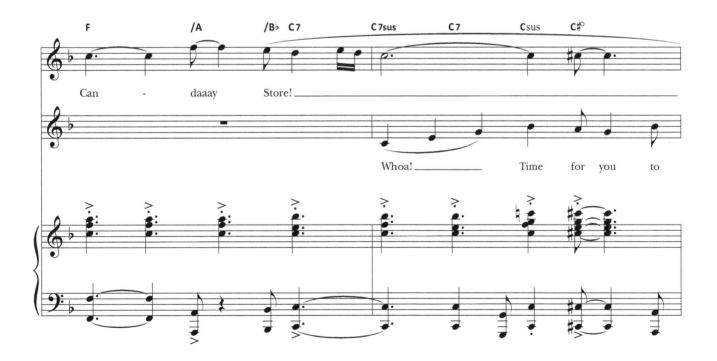

Bm7(♭5)
Gm/B♭
It's my Can - dy Store! It's my Can - dy...
It's my Can - dy Store! It's my Can - dy...
It's my Can dy Store! It's my Can - dy
It's my Can dy Store! It's my Can - dy
Store!
Store!
sffz

FIGHT FOR ME

**Music and Lyrics by
Laurence O'Keefe and Kevin Murphy**

Conversational, but not slow

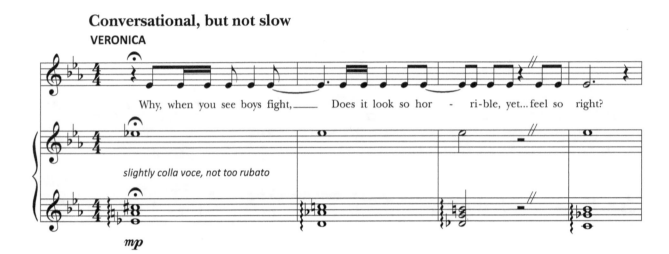

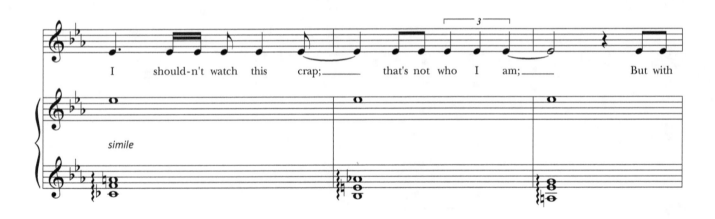

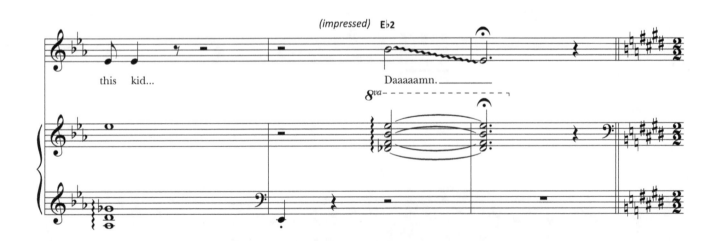

Warm andante pop ballad, non rubato

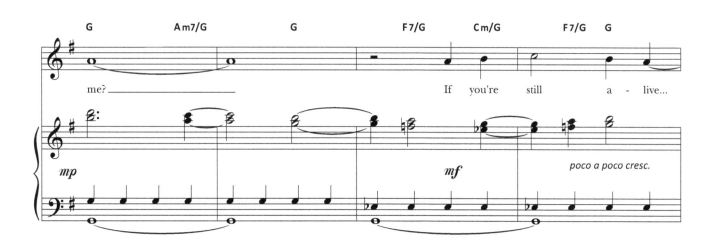

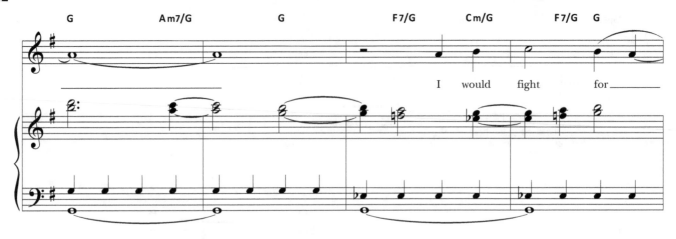

I would fight for

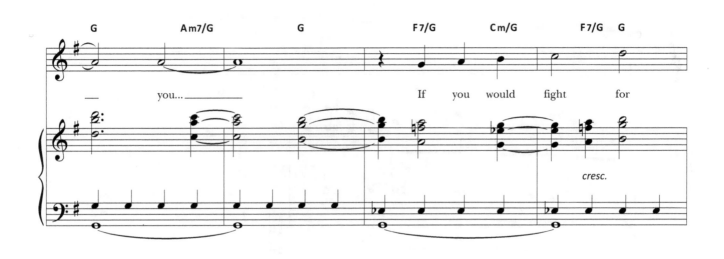

you... If you would fight for

cresc.

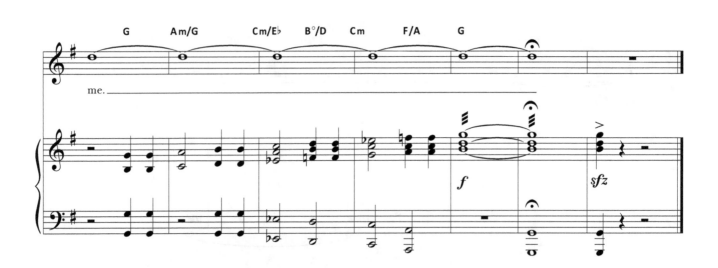

me.

f

sfz

FREEZE YOUR BRAIN

Music and Lyrics by
Laurence O'Keefe and Kevin Murphy

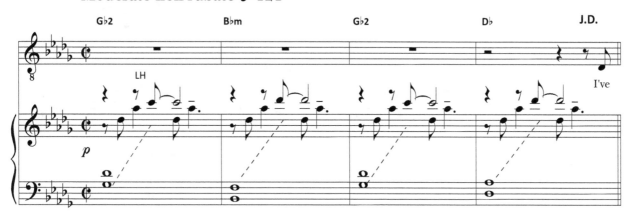

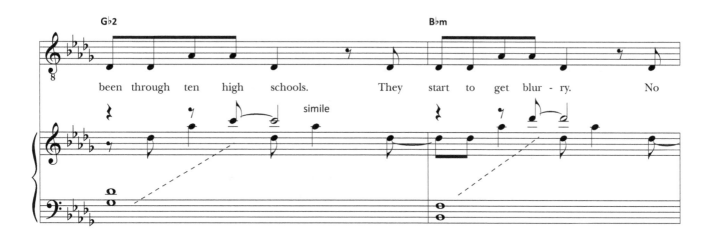

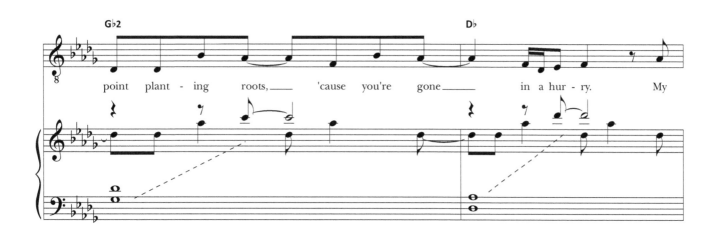

More Energy, Slightly Faster

48

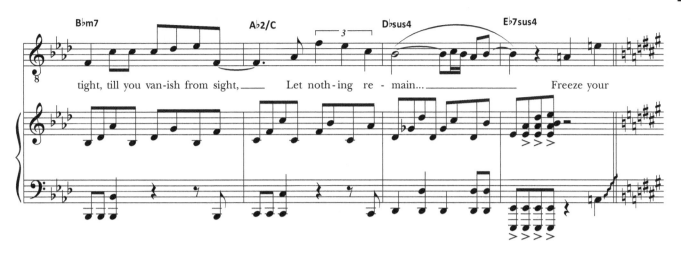

tight, till you van-ish from sight,___ Let noth-ing re - main...___ Freeze your

Hard Rock

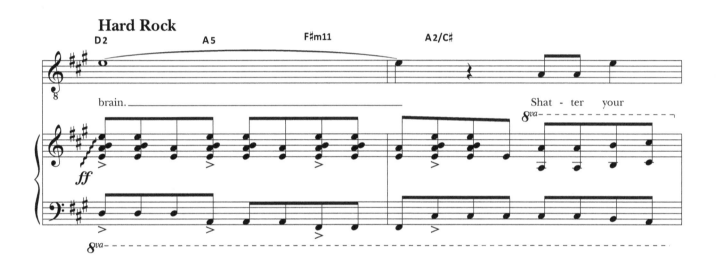

brain.___ Shat - ter your

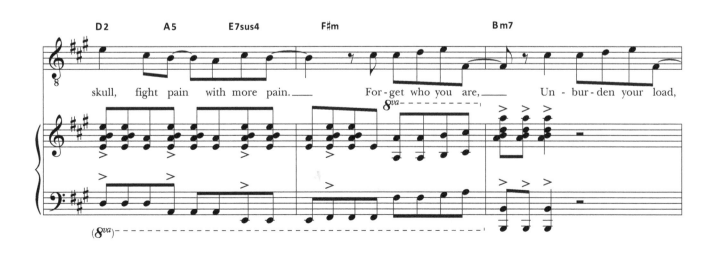

skull, fight pain with more pain.___ For - get who you are,___ Un - bur-den your load,

Forget in six weeks you'll be back on the road. When the voice in your head

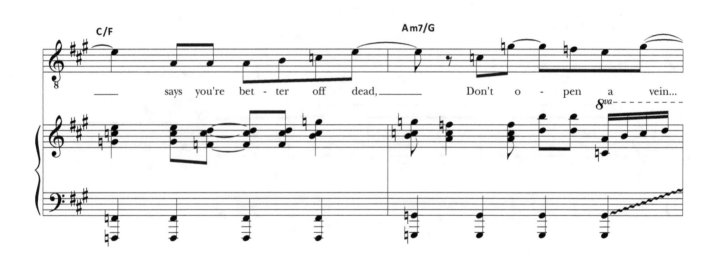

says you're better off dead, Don't open a vein...

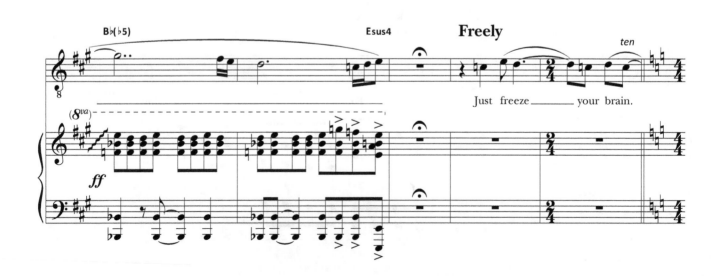

Just freeze your brain.

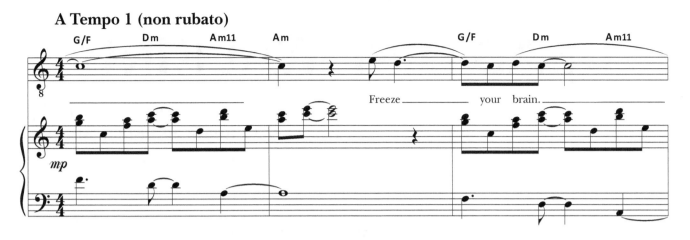

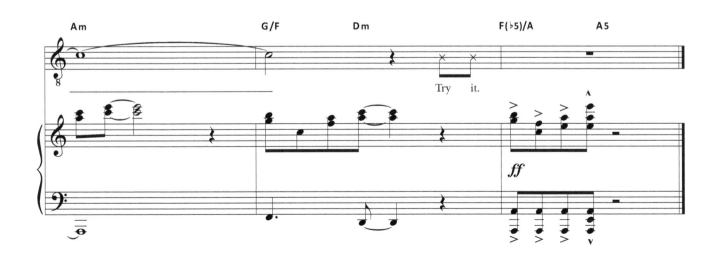

DEAD GIRL WALKING

**Music and Lyrics by
Laurence O'Keefe and Kevin Murphy**

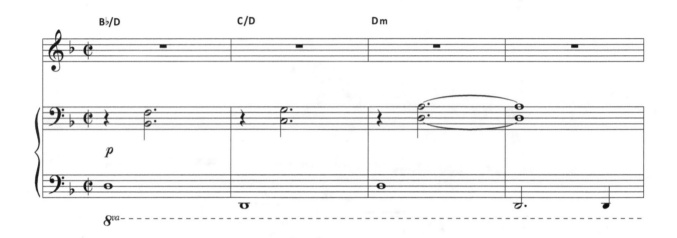

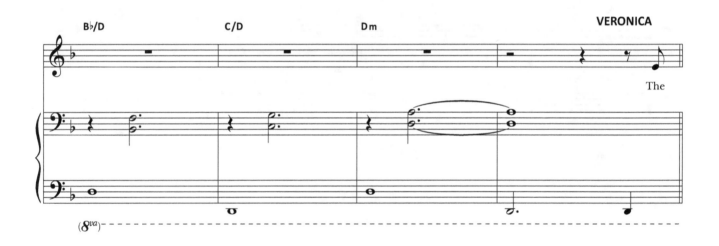

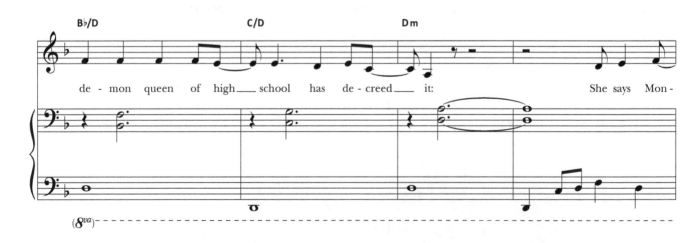

56

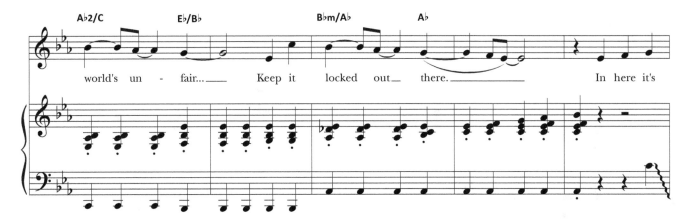

worlds un - fair... Keep it locked out there. In here it's

The Rockin' Resumes

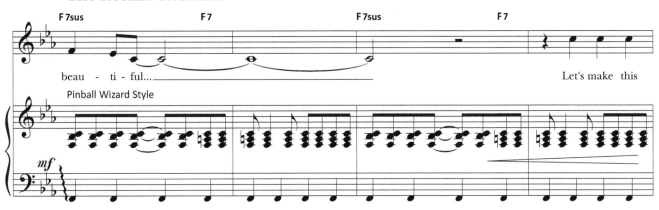

beau - ti - ful... Let's make this

beau - ti - ful! J.D.: That works for me.

60

Full-on Crazy Rockin' Out

OUR LOVE IS GOD

Music and Lyrics by
Laurence O'Keefe and Kevin Murphy

Andante, with a pulse

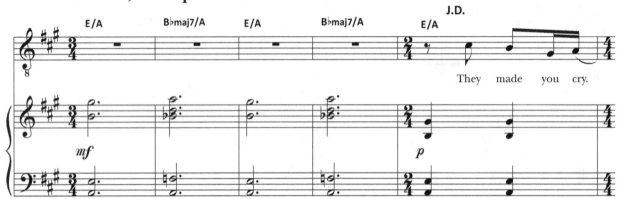

They made you cry.

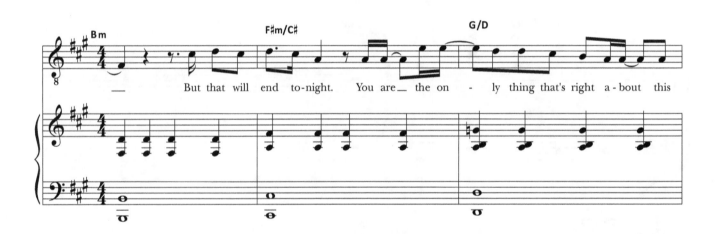

But that will end to-night. You are the on - ly thing that's right a - bout this

bro - ken world. Go on and cry, _____ But when the morn-

66

70

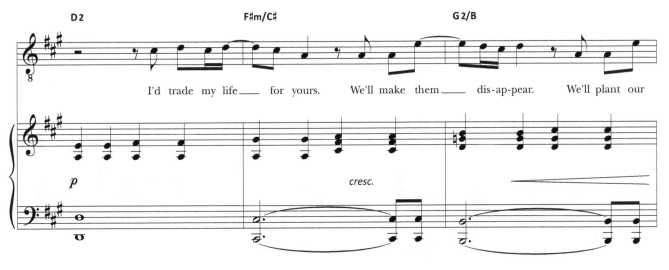

I'd trade my life___ for yours. We'll make them___ dis-ap-pear. We'll plant our

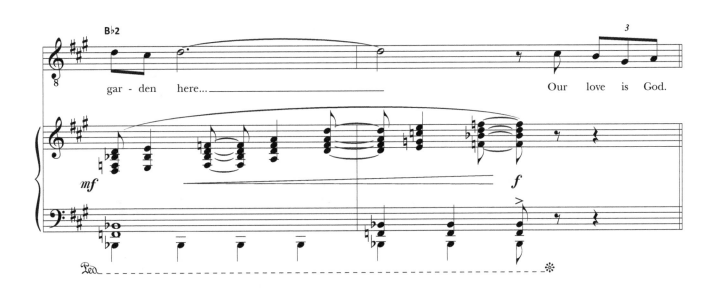

gar - den here..._____ Our love is God.

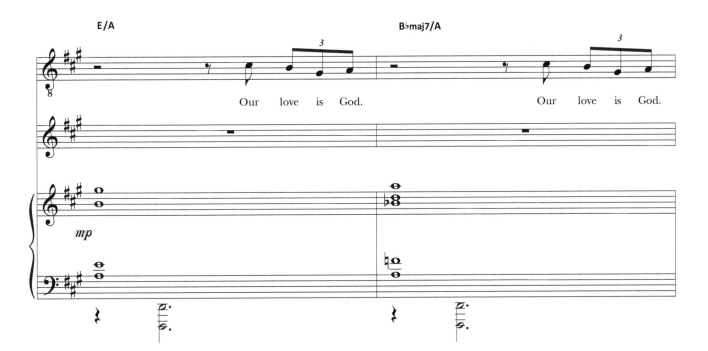

Our love is God. Our love is God.

MY DEAD GAY SON

Music and Lyrics by
Laurence O'Keefe and Kevin Murphy

A little broader

boy's a ho-mo-sex-u-al, and that don't scare me none. I

Back to Moderato, Non Rubato

want the world to know... I LOVE my dead gay

Country/Gospel 2, not too fast   RAM'S DAD. I've been thinking. Praying. Reading some magazines.

son!

RAM'S DAD. And it's time we opened our eyes.

Well, the

now I've learned___ to love...___ I love my dead gay

son!___ Now I
He loves his son. He loves his son, his dead gay son!

say my boy's in hea-ven! and he's tan-ning by the pool.___ The

Military Feel

THESE BOYS were brave as hell. THESE BOYS they knew damn well,

THOSE FOLKS would judge 'em; they were des - p'rate to be free!___

They took a reb - el stance, stripped to___ their un - der pants.

simile

RAM'S DAD

Paul, I can't be - lieve that you still re - fuse to get a clue,

83

Gospel with Double-Time Feel

SEVENTEEN

Music and Lyrics by
Laurence O'Keefe and Kevin Murphy

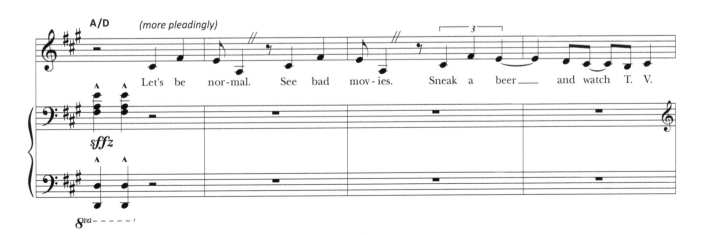

With growing warmth & energy (♩=80)

Grand Power Rock

94

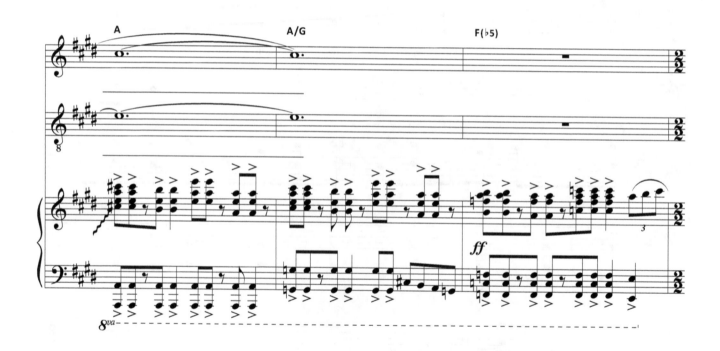

No rit or rubato. Strict 𝅗𝅥=𝅗𝅥 to end

LIFEBOAT

**Music and Lyrics by
Laurence O'Keefe and Kevin Murphy**

Mournful moderato, with a pulse (no rubato)

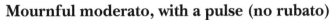

HEATHER MCNAMARA

I float in a boat

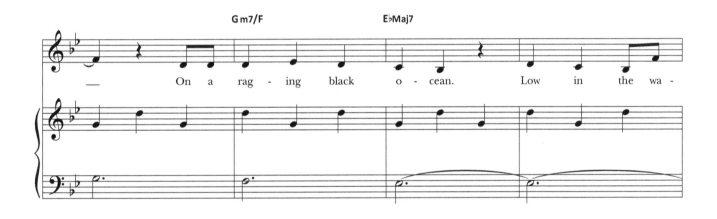

On a rag-ing black o-cean. Low in the wa-

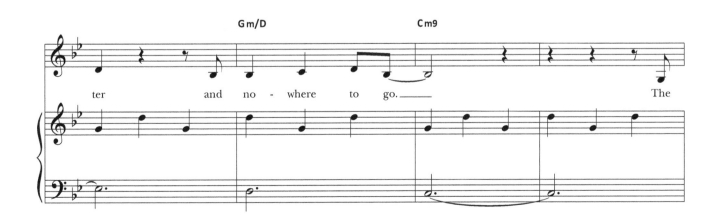

ter and no-where to go. The

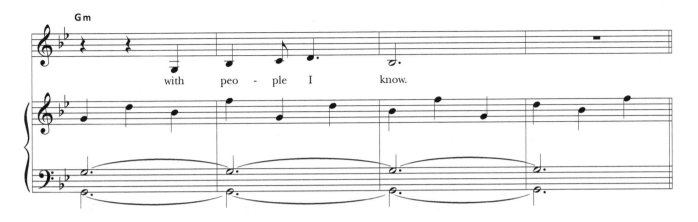

with peo - ple I know.

Sudden Loud Rock

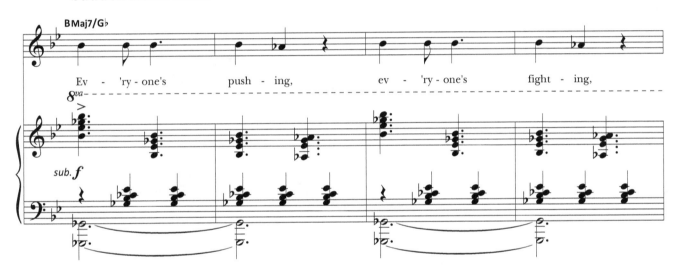

Ev - 'ry-one's push - ing, ev - 'ry-one's fight - ing,

Storms are ap - proach - ing, there's no - where to hide! _____ If I

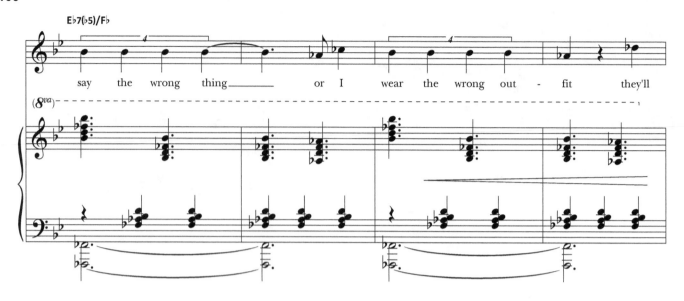

say the wrong thing____ or I wear the wrong out - fit they'll

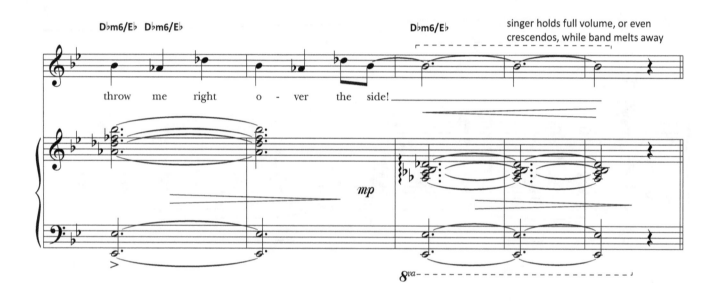

throw me right o - ver the side!____

singer holds full volume, or even
crescendos, while band melts away

Non ritard!

I'm hug - ging my knees,____ and the cap - tain is

point - ing. Well, who made her___ cap - tain? Still,

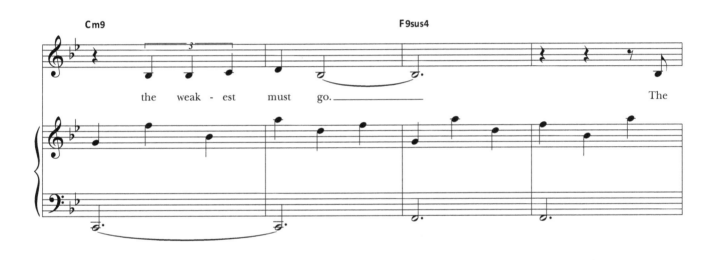

the weak - est must go.___ The

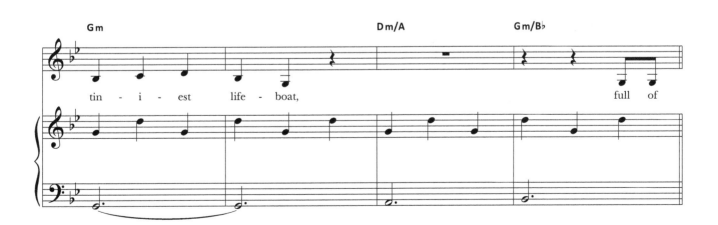

tin - i - est life - boat, full of

KINDERGARTEN BOYFRIEND

Music and Lyrics by
Laurence O'Keefe and Kevin Murphy

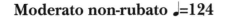

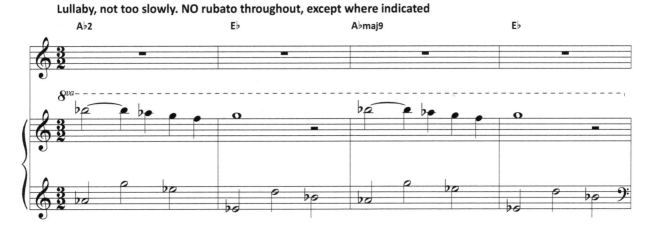

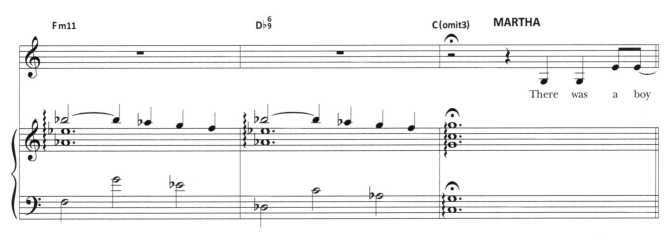

Gentle, slow but steady. Absolutely NO rubato.
(So vocals can float a bit)

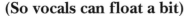

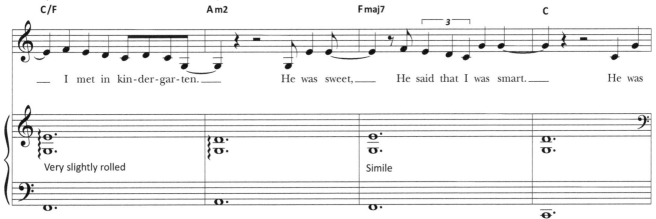

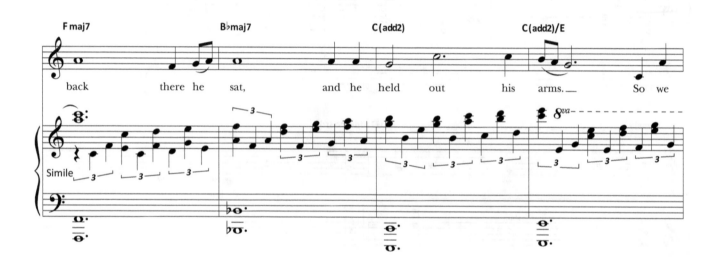

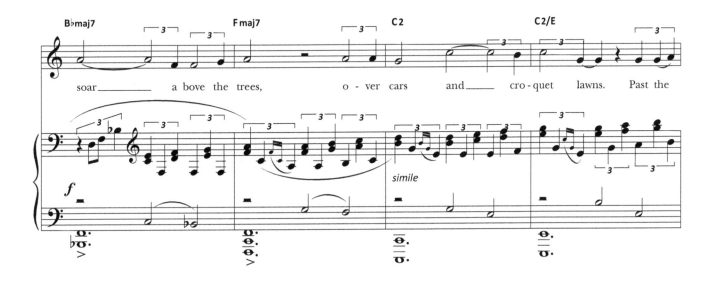

110

MEANT TO BE YOURS

Music and Lyrics by
Laurence O'Keefe and Kevin Murphy

Gleefully

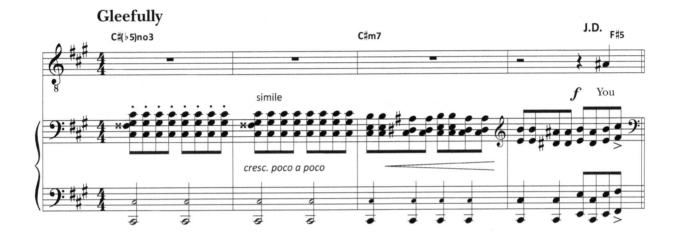

chucked me out__ like I__ was trash, for that__ you should be dead. But! But! But!

Then it hit__ me like__ a flash, What if high school went__ a - way in - stead?

118

SEVENTEEN (REPRISE)

**Music and Lyrics by
Laurence O'Keefe and Kevin Murphy**

We'll en-dure___ it. We'll sur-vive___ it. Mar-tha, are you free to-night?

MARTHA. What?
VERONICA. My date for the pep rally kind of blew... me off. So I was wondering if you weren't doing anything tonight, maybe we could pop some Jiffy Pop, rent some new releases? Something with a happy ending?
MARTHA. <u>Are</u> there any happy endings?

Play 3x

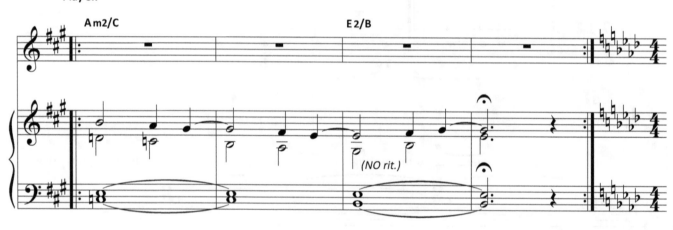

Gently

I can't prom-ise no more Heath-ers. High school may not e-ver end.

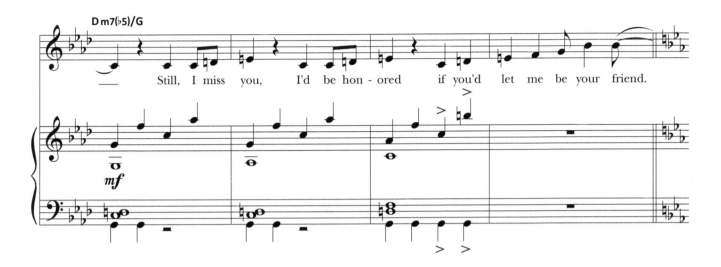

Still, I miss you, I'd be hon-ored if you'd let me be your friend.

Gentle Groove

VERONICA

We can be sev - en - teen.

MARTHA

My friend...

We can be sev - en - teen.

VERONICA and MARTHA

We can learn how___ to chill.

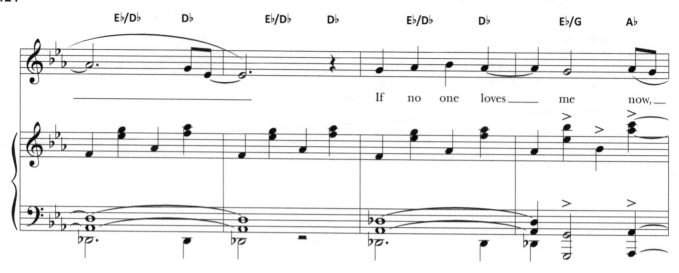

If no one loves___ me now,

Some - day some - bo - - dy___ will.

accel. poco a poco

A tiny bit faster, with growing energy

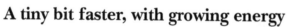

(will.)_____ We can be sev - en - teen.

Still time to make_____ things right.

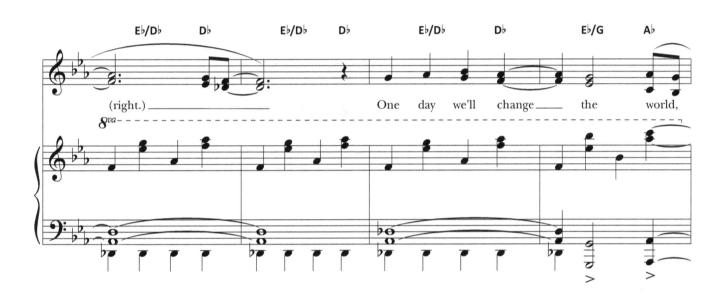

(right.)_____ One day we'll change_____ the world,

_____ but let's kick back_____ to - night!

accel poco a poco

We are now definitely rockin'. A bit faster and harder

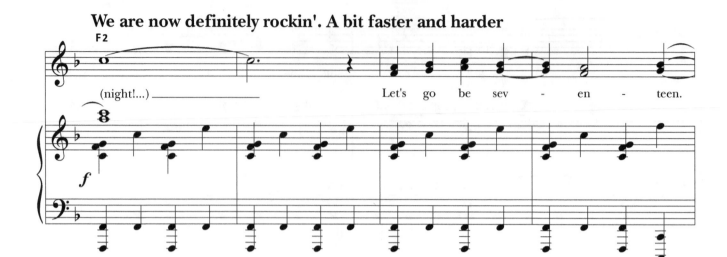

(night!...) _____ Let's go be sev - en - teen.

_____ Take off our clothes___ and dance.

(dance.) _____ Act like we're all___ still kids.___

Accel...

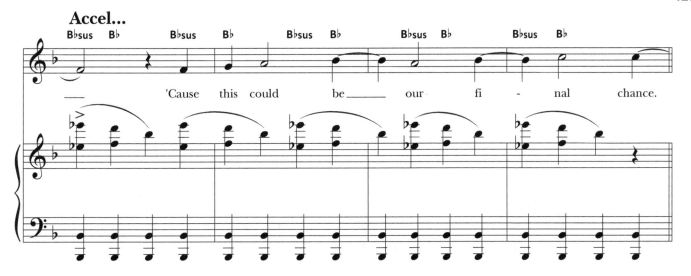

'Cause this could be ___ our fi - nal chance.

The rockin' has escalated

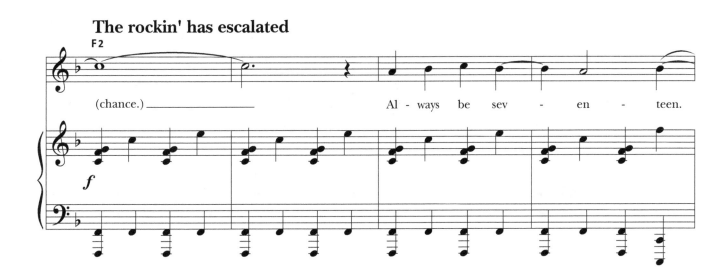

(chance.) ___ Al - ways be sev - en - teen.

___ Cel - e - brate, you ___ and I.

(I.) _____ May - be we won't___ grow old,___

F/A   Bb

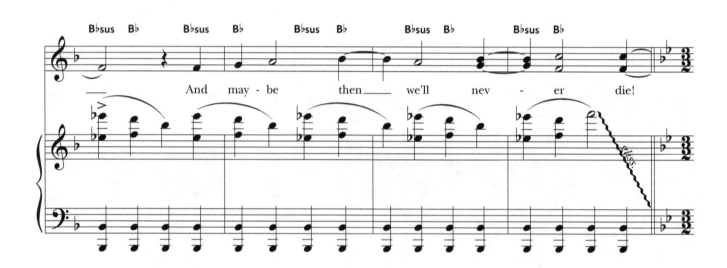

And may - be then___ we'll nev - er die!

Bbsus Bb   Bbsus Bb   Bbsus Bb   Bbsus Bb   Bbsus Bb

Very fast hard rock ♩=♩ (no more accelerandos; steady tempo til end)

Gb(b5)   Ebm7   Bbsus Bb   Bbsus Bb   Bbsus Bb   Bbsus Bb

(die!) _____   We'll make it___ beau - ti - ful!

ff   *f*

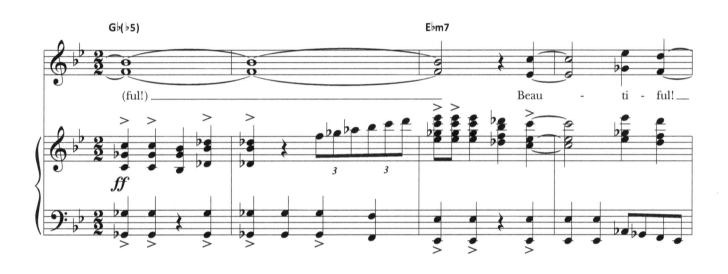

130

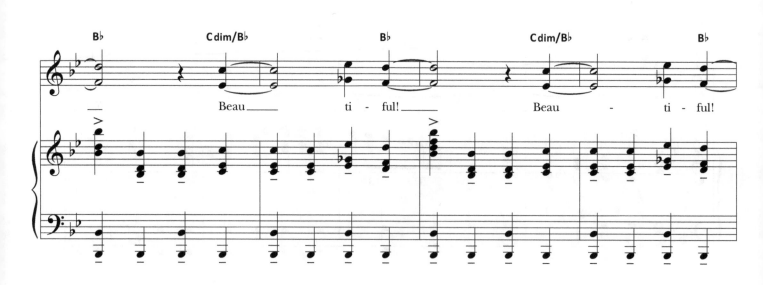

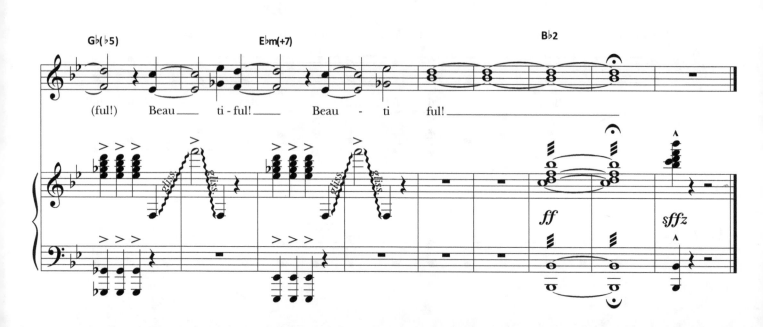

CREATORS

LAURENCE O'KEEFE (*Book*, *Music* and *Lyrics*) was a producer of the original LA and NY productions of *Heathers The Musical* (Drama Desk nom for music). With his wife, Nell Benjamin, he won the Olivier Award (London's Tony) for co-writing *Legally Blonde: The Musical*, which ran two and a half years on the West End and has toured the UK and Ireland. *Blonde* received seven Tony Award nominations, two US national tours, and several international productions, winning Australia's Helpmann Award for Best Musical. Larry wrote the Off-Broadway smash *Bat Boy: The Musical*, which won the Lucille Lortel Award, two Richard Rodgers Awards, and the New York Outer Critics Circle Award for Best Musical, and has received over five hundred productions worldwide, including productions in the West End, Tokyo, Seoul, Berlin, and Edinburgh.

Larry has composed music and/or lyrics for *The Daily Show*, SyFy's *Defiance*, the Disney Channel, PBS, and Cirque du Soleil. Recent projects include *Julie's Greenroom* for Netflix, NBC's *Best Time Ever with Neil Patrick Harris*, and ITV's *Ant & Dec's Saturday Night Takeaway*. Upcoming projects with Nell Benjamin include *Life Of The Party*, set in the movie musical industry in Stalin's Soviet Union, and *Huzzah!*, an epic romantic musical comedy about love, betrayal, demagoguery, dictatorship, and revolution at a Renaissance Faire.

Larry is the winner of the Ed Kleban Award for lyrics, a Jonathan Larson Grant, and the ASCAP Richard Rodgers New Horizon Award. A graduate of Harvard and USC, Larry teaches master classes at Harvard, Yale, NYU, and elsewhere.

KEVIN MURPHY (*Book*, *Music* and *Lyrics*) was a producer of the original LA and NY productions of *Heathers The Musical* (Drama Desk nom for music). He also provided lyrics and co-wrote the book for the stage musical *Reefer Madness* and was a producer for both the Los Angeles premiere and Off-Broadway productions. *Reefer* swept the three major Los Angeles theatre awards, which included triple wins for Best Musical and Best Score. In New York, Kevin's lyrics were nominated for a Drama Desk Award. Kevin co-adapted *Reefer* into a Showtime Original movie which premiered at the 2005 Sundance Film Festival and screened in competition at the 2005 Deauville Film Festival, winning the Premiere Audience Award. The movie received three Emmy nominations, winning for Outstanding Music & Lyrics.

Kevin is also a television creator/writer/producer. He is the showrunner for the current AMC series *The Son*, a historical drama starring Pierce Brosnan. Other TV writing credits include: *Desperate Housewives* (Golden Globe winner, two-time WGA Award nom, Emmy nom); *Defiance* (co-creator/showrunner); *Ed*; *Reaper*; *Caprica* (showrunner); *Valentine* (co-creator/showrunner); *Hellcats* (co-creator/showrunner); *Honey, I Shrunk the Kids* (syndicated series, co-creator/showrunner).

CPSIA information can be obtained
at www.ICGtesting.com
Printed in the USA
BVHW01s1753071018
529510BV00006B/146/P